# The Runaway Watermelon

Rhea G. Madison James

The Runaway Watermelon

iUniverse books may be ordered through booksellers or by contacting:

iUniverse
1663 Liberty Drive
Bloomington, IN 47403
www.iuniverse.com
1-800-Authors (1-800-288-4677)

ISBN: 978-1-5320-9681-5 (sc)
ISBN: 978-1-5320-9682-2 (e)

Library of Congress Control Number: 2020904314

Print information available on the last page.

iUniverse rev. date: 03/04/2020

# The Runaway Watermelon

A long, long time ago, there were people in a small village, and they did not have any food. All they had was a watermelon. Anabella and Max were friends who lived in this village. They were really hungry. In the small village, there was a runaway watermelon.

"run run run as fast as you can! You can't catch me because Im the watermelon Man."

Max and Anabella jumped and jumped after the Watermelon Man. They passed one bee.

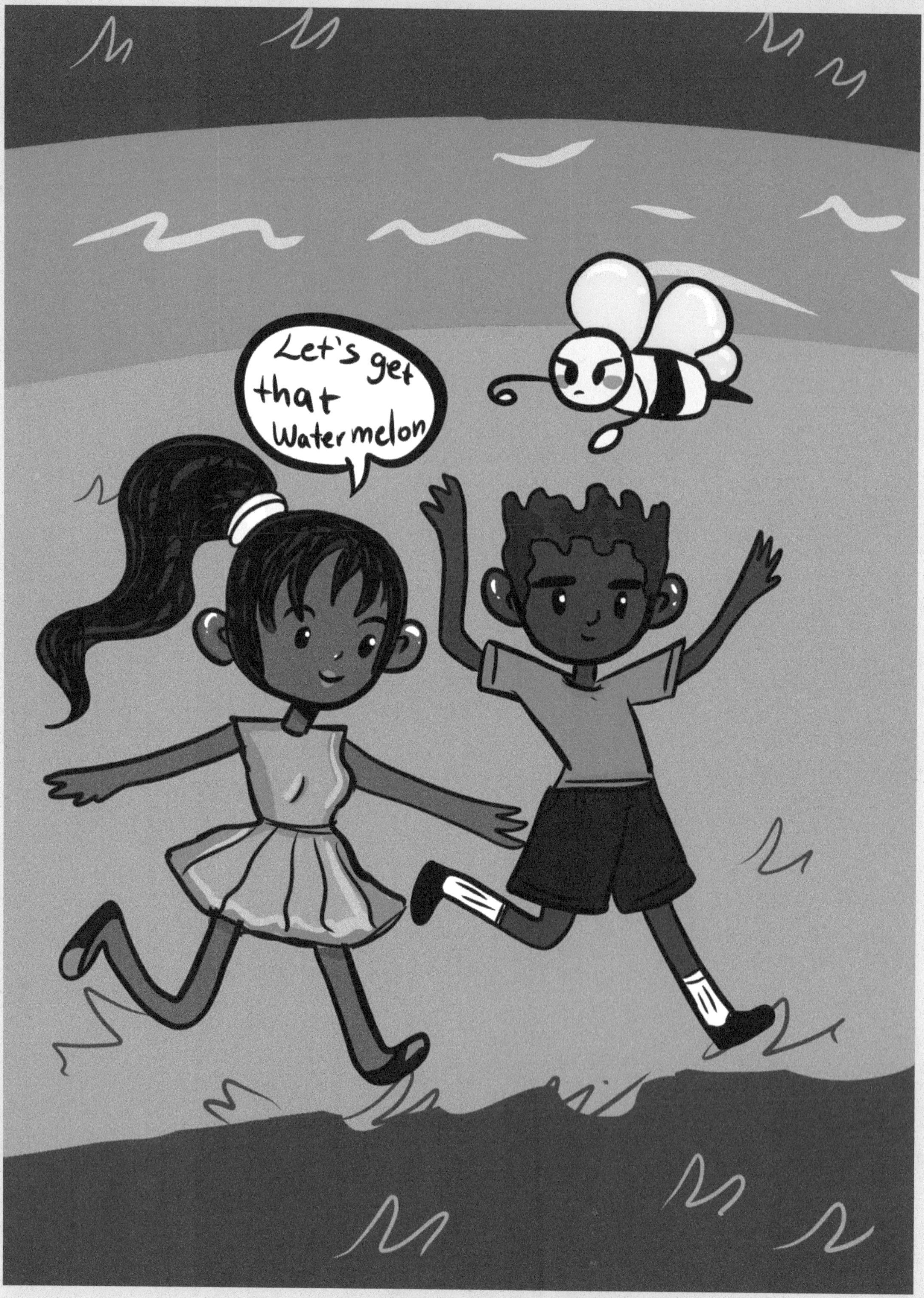
Let's get that Watermelon

The bee stung the Watermelon Man, but nothing stopped the Watermelon Man from running away.

Anabella acted like she was poor so the Watermelon Man can feel sad.

The Watermelon Man ran as fast as a race car. Next, the Watermelon Man got mad and he sang, "Run, run, run as fast as you can. You can't catch me because I'm the Watermelon Man!"

Then the Watermelon Man crashed. Zoom! Anabella said, "vroom, vroom."

Max said, "Whoosh".

The Watermelon Man seemed dead. Anabella and Max were sad. They began to cry and ate some of the Watermelon. The Watermelon Man got up and he became bigger and angrier.

He was a Watermelon Monster. Anabella and Max knew they could not handle the Watermelon Monster. They needed help so the Watermelon Monster didn't smash the village.

Four frogs jumped onto the Watermelon Monster. Suddenly, six ponies chased the Watermelon Monster. Then, Donald Trump came, and he said, "I would like to banish the Watermelon Monster."

Then Barack Obama came, and he said, "I would like to catch this Watermelon Monster," but he was not able to do so.

The Bryan/Roach Team, Governor and Lt. Governor of the Virgin Islands said, "We will trash this Watermelon Monster to get him out of this village." And they did! They saved the village, and everyone was happy again.

# About the Author

My name is Rhea G. Madison James. I
was born on June 1, 2011, on the beautiful
island of St. Thomas US Virgin Islands.
I have one sibling named Ricky James Jr.

I am a 3rd grade student who enjoys
dancing, karate, tennis, and writing.

I love to give and believe everyone should
treat people the way they want to be treated.

This book is dedicated to my parents
Ricky Sr. and Trisha James

# About the Illustrator

Deja-Marie Simon is a high school student at the Virgin Islands Montessori School and Peter Gruber International Academy on St. Thomas USVI. From the age of four she started molding items out of clay and making dolly clothing out of fishing wire. She enjoys drawing, painting, and digital art.

Her dream career is to become an Illustrator or an Art Director. This was her first illustration and she will continue to work with young authors to gain more experience.

Both the Author and Illustrator are from
St. Thomas, U.S. Virgin Islands.

CPSIA information can be obtained
at www.ICGtesting.com
Printed in the USA
LVHW071314110122
708283LV00023B/595

9 781532 096815